BBC Children's Books
Published by the Penguin Group
Penguin Books Ltd, 80 Strand, London, WC2R 0RL, England
Penguin Group (USA) Inc., 375 Hudson Street, New York 10014, USA
Penguin Books (Australia) Ltd, 250 Camberwell Road, Camberwell,
Victoria 3124, Australia
(A division of Pearson Australia Group PTY Ltd)
Penguin Group (NZ), 67 Apollo Drive, Rosedale, Auckland
0632, New Zealand (a division of Pearson New Zealand Ltd)
Canada, India, South Africa
Published by BBC Children's Books, 2011
Text and design © Children's Character Books
Illustrations by Jamie Smart
001 - 10 9 8 7 6 5 4 3 2 1

BBC logo © BBC 1996. Doctor Who logo © BBC 2009. TARDIS image © BBC 1963.
Dalek image © BBC/Terry Nation 1963. Cyberman image © BBC/Kit Pedler/Gerry
Davies 1966. K-9 image © BBC/Bob Baker/Dave Martin 1977.
Licensed by BBC Worldwide Limited
BBC, DOCTOR WHO (word marks, logos and devices), TARDIS, DALEKS,
CYBERMAN and K-9 (word marks and devices) are trade marks of the British
Broadcasting Corporation and are used under licence.

ISBN: 9781405908177
Printed in Italy

Contents

Where *is* the Doctor?

The Doctor is an intergalactic man of mystery, travelling through time and space, never knowing where he will end up from one day to the next. His faithful ship and oldest friend, the TARDIS, takes him wherever he needs to go – sometimes the Doctor can control the destination, but more often the TARDIS decides and transports him to wherever he is needed most.

Many have tried to find the Doctor, from human organisations like L.I.N.D.A and Torchwood, to the Shadow Proclamation and all manner of alien enemies who want to destroy the Time Lord. They've followed his progress over hundreds of years, tracking him around the world and across the galaxies.

Spotter's List

The following things can be found in every scene:

The Doctor	The TARDIS	Amy Pond	Rory Williams

Some have even laid traps for him and, at times, have been successful in catching him. But there's one thing you must never do, and that is put the Doctor in a trap. The Doctor won't be held for long and always escapes to fight another day, continuing on his endless journey through the stars.

Enclosed in these pages are just a few of the places the Doctor has visited. Amy Pond and Rory Williams are hiding here with him, along with his TARDIS. There are also many other things to search for on page 34.

Can you succeed where many have failed and find them?

Tricky Spotter's List

The following things can be found somewhere in the book:

Fido the Dog

Fido's dinner

Fido's Ball

Judoon on the Moon

There are many Judoon upon the moon, but where's the Doctor?

Dalek Ship

A ship packed with Daleks is a very dangerous place for the Doctor and Amy Pond to be hanging out! Can you spot him before they exterminate him?

Adipose Nursery Ship

These cute little critters are having a party. Can you see their uninvited guests?

Cyberfactory

Find the Time Lord
and his friends before the
Cybermen delete them!

Byzantium Forest

Whatever you do, don't blink until you've found the Doctor and his friends among the trees.

The Ood-Sphere

The Ood are generally pretty friendly, until they turn red-eyed! Can you find the Doctor and his friends before the Ood are possessed?

Sontaran Boot Camp

They might be highly trained soldiers, but the Sontarans haven't spotted the Doctor and his friends yet. Can you?

The Underhenge

The Doctor's enemies are out in force. Can you find him before they trap him in the Pandorica?

Saturnyne

Seek out the Doctor, Amy and Rory in this undersea city of the Saturnynes.

The Silence

Watch out for the Silence as you search for the Doctor, Amy and Rory.

The Slitheen

Can you find the Doctor,
Amy and Rory in the time
it takes the Slitheen to spell
Raxacoricofallapatorius?

Silurian City

There's no time to hibernate when the Doctor is lost in the underground city of the Silurians with Amy and Rory!

More to find...

Judoon on the Moon

- [ ] Sunbathing Judoon
- [ ] Four US astronauts
- [ ] Drilling Judoon
- [ ] Judoon riding on a rocket
- [ ] Judoon on a bike
- [ ] Two Judoon playing chess
- [ ] Judoon holding an oar
- [ ] Green sweet
- [ ] Two Judoon boxing
- [ ] 'Wanted dead or alive' poster

Dalek Ship

- [ ] Cyberman head on a wall plaque
- [ ] Box of monkeys
- [ ] Dalek reading a newspaper
- [ ] Doctor target practice
- [ ] Two Weeping Angels
- [ ] Portrait of Davros
- [ ] Dalek Supreme (not on a screen)
- [ ] K-9
- [ ] Open Dalek Strategist casing
- [ ] Jammie Dodger

Adipose Nursery Ship

- [ ] Adipose in a spacesuit
- [ ] Adipose with an umbrella
- [ ] Clown balloon
- [ ] Adipose with a giant lollipop
- [ ] Adipose in star-shaped glasses
- [ ] Eight Adipose nurses
- [ ] Adipose DJ
- [ ] Pan on fire
- [ ] Adipose with a spanner
- [ ] Two Adipose playing tennis

Cyberfactory

- [ ] Pirate
- [ ] 'Robot disco 9pm' sign
- [ ] Sleeping Cyberman
- [ ] Teddy bear
- [ ] Cyberman wearing a suit and tie
- [ ] Clown
- [ ] Two Cybermen playing football
- [ ] Cyberman selling ice creams
- [ ] Winder
- [ ] Cyberman eating toast

Byzantium Forest

- [ ] Two squirrels
- [ ] Eight Clerics
- [ ] Kite
- [ ] Weeping Angel wearing the Doctor's jacket
- [ ] A tree with two apples
- [ ] Two-headed Angel
- [ ] Beehive
- [ ] Weeping Angel in a tree stump
- [ ] Weeping Angel fallen over
- [ ] Jamie Smart's signature

The Ood-Sphere

- [ ] Ood Sigma
- [ ] Two snow-Ood
- [ ] Ood with its tongue stuck to a lamp pos
- [ ] Ood wearing a purple bobble hat
- [ ] Igloo
- [ ] Ood fishing in a hole
- [ ] Surfing Ood
- [ ] Red-eyed Ood
- [ ] Penguin
- [ ] Blue flag

Sontaran Boot Camp

- [ ] Sontaran wearing a rubber ring
- [ ] Hula-hooping Sontaran
- [ ] Cake with a cherry on the top
- [ ] Sontaran holding a red flag
- [ ] Sontaran with a green balloon
- [ ] Rutan spy with binoculars
- [ ] Sontaran lifting weights
- [ ] Three Sontarans in green boats
- [ ] Sontaran diving off a springboard
- [ ] Green clone

The Underhenge

- [ ] Sontaran in a 'Kiss the Cook' apron
- [ ] Judoon on a trampoline
- [ ] Roman thinking about potatoes
- [ ] Cyberman dressed as the Doctor
- [ ] Lobster
- [ ] Roman eating a burger
- [ ] Cyberman knitting
- [ ] Fez
- [ ] Sontaran with a spider
- [ ] Silurian blowing up a balloon

Saturnyne

- [ ] Saturnyne carrying a swag bag
- [ ] Apple on a sword
- [ ] Saturnyne catching a star in a net
- [ ] Two smiling starfish
- [ ] Saturnyne with an umbrella
- [ ] Two Saturnyne having a picnic
- [ ] Seahorse
- [ ] Burping Saturnyne
- [ ] Unhappy fish
- [ ] Jar of fish food

The Silence

- [ ] Ginger cat
- [ ] Silent in an astronaut helmet
- [ ] Yellow car
- [ ] Astronaut
- [ ] Snake
- [ ] Two chessboards
- [ ] Slinky
- [ ] Silent in a puddle
- [ ] Toybox
- [ ] Man drawing on the wall

The Slitheen

- [ ] Melting snowman
- [ ] Slitheen reading a book
- [ ] Yellow duck
- [ ] Slitheen lifeguard
- [ ] Slitheen with a slingshot
- [ ] Two Slitheen having a water fight
- [ ] Slitheen wearing a shark fin
- [ ] Slitheen blowing a fish into the air
- [ ] Discarded human costume
- [ ] Two Slitheen firing brooms with bows

Silurian City

- [ ] Silurian with a teddy bear
- [ ] Three Silurians playing basketball
- [ ] Silurian driving a remote-controlled car
- [ ] Silurian tipping a bucket of water over another Silurian
- [ ] Five tongue-tied Silurians
- [ ] Silurian wearing safari clothes
- [ ] Silurian Elder
- [ ] Silurian with a yo-yo
- [ ] Silurian dropping a packet of crisps
- [ ] Silurian reading a book

There are ten differences between these pictures. Can you spot them?

Other great *Doctor Who* books to collect

DOCTOR WHO BBC
100 SCARIEST MONSTERS

POSTCARDS FROM TIME AND SPACE
100 DOCTOR WHO POSTCARDS IN ONE BOX

NEW! A MUST-HAVE FOR ALL WHERE'S THE DOCTOR? FANS

SUBSCRIBE TODAY!

AND GET 2 ISSUES FOR ONLY £5.20 A MONTH!

Collect the awesome new *Doctor Who Monster Invasion* and build up a mega-monster magazine and cool trading card collection!

DON'T MISS!
Fantastic NEW Where's The Doctor? puzzle in every issue

✓ Every issue comes with a pack of trading cards!

✓ Packed with cool alien facts, monster slamdowns and puzzles!

✓ Learn how to play brilliant games with your cards at www.doctorwhomi.com

✓ Bring your 3-D cards to life and unlock brilliant game bonuses!

BBC THE ULTIMATE MAGAZINE AND TRADING CARD COLLECTION
DOCTOR WHO MONSTER INVASION
www.doctorwhomi.com PART 1

BATTLE OF THE DALEKS
WHO WILL WIN?

INSIDE!
CAN YOU FIND THE DOCTOR?

CYBERMEN · PRISONER ZERO · AMY POND

DOCTOR WHO MONSTER INVASION
OFFICIAL TRADING CARD GAME

VISIT **www.doctorwhomi.com/subscribe** ENTER CODE WTDB

CALL THE HOTLINE NOW **0871 277 0190** QUOTE CODE WTDB